SIMON & SCHUSTER BOOKS FOR YOUNG READERS • An imprint of Simon & Schuster Children's Publishing Division • 1230 Avenue of the Americas, New York, New York 10020 • © 1992 by Tomie dePaola • Book design by Laurent Linn © 2021 by Simon & Schuster, Inc. • All rights reserved, including the right of reproduction in whole or in part in any form. • SIMON & SCHUSTER BOOKS FOR YOUNG READERS and related marks are trademarks of Simon & Schuster, Inc. • For information about special discounts for bulk purchases, please contact Simon & Schuster Special Sales at 1-866-506-1949 or business@simonandschuster.com. • The Simon & Schuster Speakers Bureau can bring authors to your live event. For more information or to book an event, contact the Simon & Schuster Speakers Bureau at 1-866-248-3049 or visit our website at www.simonspeakers.com. • The text for this book was set in Dutch Mediaeval. • The illustrations for this book were rendered in acrylics. • Manufactured in China • 0621 SCP • First Edition • 2 4 6 8 10 9 7 5 3 1 • Library of Congress Cataloging-in-Publication Data • Names: DePaola, Tomie, 1934– author, illustrator. • Title: Jingle the Christmas clown / Tomie dePaola. • Description: First edition. | New York : Simon & Schuster Books for Young Readers, [2021] | Audience: Ages 4–8. | Audience: Grades K–1. | Summary: Staying behind when their circus moves on, a young clown and a troupe of baby animals put on a special Christmas Eve show for an Italian village too poor to celebrate the holiday. • Identifiers: LCCN 2020031900 (print) | LCCN 2020031901 (ebook) | ISBN 9781534466562 (hardcover) | ISBN 9781534466586 (ebook) • Subjects: CYAC: Clowns—Fiction. | Circus—Fiction. | Christmas—Fiction. | Animals—Infancy—Fiction. | Italy—Fiction. • Classification: LCC PZ7.D439 Ji 2021 (print) | LCC PZ7.D439 (ebook) | DDC [E]—dc23 • LC record available at https://lccn.loc.gov/2020031900 • LC ebook record available at https://lccn.loc.gov/2020031901

JINGLE
THE CHRISTMAS CLOWN

Story and Pictures by

TOMIE dePAOLA

Simon & Schuster Books for Young Readers

New York   London   Toronto   Sydney   New Delhi

For Timmie Poh,
who does so much
for the young people
in New London, NH;

and for Bob Hechtel,
who does so much
for me and Whitebird.

Oom-pah-pah. Oom-pah-pah.
Rat-a-tat-tat. Rat-a-tat-tat.
Oom-pah-pah. Oom-pah-pah.
Tiddily-tiddily-dee. Tiddily-tiddily-dee.
Oom-pah-pah. Oom-pah-pah.

Nothing sounded happier to Jingle than the music of the band filling the air as *Il Circo Piccolo*—The Little Circus— traveled across the countryside.

Jingle rode with the baby animals. The older clowns said that he was still too young and small to perform with them, so it was Jingle's job to take care of the babies.

"Frick, Frack, Smick, and Smack, be still," he called to the baby monkeys, who were jumping back and forth between Sparkle, the pony, and Pita, the donkey. The baby elephant's trunk drooped. "Don't worry, Lolly, we'll be there soon and you can rest."

Every year *Il Circo Piccolo* stopped at the same village before
going on to the big city, where it performed from the day after
Natale—Christmas—until *Capodanno*—New Year's Day. On
the *vigilia di Natale*—Christmas Eve—there would be a special
show for the village. It was Jingle's favorite night. All the villagers,
young and old, laughed and clapped and cheered.

"There's the village!" the impresario shouted out.

"It looks different," said Madame Sophie, the bareback rider. "There's no smoke coming out of the chimneys."

"Everything looks closed up," said Rollo, the tightrope walker.

A cold gust of wind blew across the hills, and the aerialist family shivered. "Where is everyone?" they asked.

As the circus troupe looked on, a small group of people climbed up the hill to meet them.

"*Buon giorno*, Signor Mayor," greeted the impresario. "*Il Circo Piccolo* is here once again, ready to perform on Christmas Eve."

"Ah, impresario," the mayor said, puffing from his climb. "I have sad news. I'm afraid there can be no circus this year. Too much rain in the spring and a hot, dry summer have ruined our crops, and many families have left our village. There is hardly anyone here."

"Our little mill has stopped," the miller's wife said. "My husband had to go to another town to look for work."

"Only we *vecchietti*"—old timers—"are left," Pietro, the barber, told them. "Most of our shops have closed."

"Even the church has closed," said Signora Lena, who used to clean the priest's house. "We have to go all the way to the next town for the Holy Mass."

"So we won't be celebrating Christmas here this year," the mayor added sadly. "And we certainly can't afford the circus either. We're sorry, everyone."

"This is terrible," the impresario said.

"What shall we do?" asked the clowns Toto and Clippo.

"Let's keep going to the city," said Il Muscolo, the strongman. "If we hurry we can get the tents up and do a Christmas Eve performance there."

"Yes, yes, you're right," the impresario agreed. "Let's get moving, everyone. *Arrivederci*, my friends. We are sorry for your troubles and we hope that next year things will be better for you."

"Impresario, sir," a small voice said. It was Jingle.

"What is it, Jingle?" the impresario asked.

"The baby animals, signore. They are too tired and too small to go all that way now. We have been traveling all day. Can't we rest here tonight and go tomorrow?"

"If we wait, we'll lose too much time," Il Muscolo complained.

"Let Jingle stay here with the babies. We can come back for them after the Christmas Eve performance," Madame Sophie suggested.

"It's only the day after tomorrow," said Toto and Clippo.

"Will you be all right, Jingle?" the impresario asked. The little clown nodded sadly.

"Jingle, you can set up your tent near my barn," offered Donna
Chiara. Every winter she let the circus stay in her fields.

"We will help," some of the old people said. "A small tent shouldn't
be too hard."

So it was decided. *Il Circo Piccolo* would move on, and Jingle and
the baby animals would stay behind. Jingle watched as the wagons
rode away. Poor Jingle. Poor baby animals. They all tried not to cry.

In no time a small tent was pitched for Jingle and the babies, and their wagon was parked nearby. Jingle got food and water for them all.

Donna Chiara came out to them. "Well, *bambini miei*"—my children— she said. "I am sorry that you have to be here in our sad little village, especially with Christmas coming. Nobody young, not even baby animals, should be without Christmas."

"But what about you and all the others?" Jingle asked. "Won't you miss Christmas?"

"We old folks have had many Christmases before," Donna Chiara said with a smile, "and the priest is coming on Christmas Day to celebrate the Holy Mass. But I will miss our Mass on the *vigilia di Natale*," she said sadly, "and everyone will miss the family feasts that night, and the *stelline d'oro*, our special cookies that look like golden stars. But we have our memories, so it won't be too bad."

But Jingle saw the tears in her eyes.

"Well, *buonanotte, piccini*"—good night, little ones—Donna Chiara said, and she went into her home.

Now Jingle began to feel sorrier for the villagers than for himself and the baby animals.

"It's so sad, babies," Jingle said to the animals. "I can't even imagine *no* Christmas! I wish there were something we could do for our friends."

The baby animals gathered around him. Arfur and Bowsie, the puppies, hopped up onto Jingle's lap. Rana, the tiger cub, and Simbo, the lion cub, snuggled next to him. Even Frick, Frack, Smick, and Smack stopped chasing each other around and looked at Jingle.

Suddenly Arfur and Bowsie jumped down and began to dance around like the big dogs. Lolly stood on her hind legs, while the cubs swatted their paws like the big cats.

"That's it," Jingle cried. "We will put on a circus of our own for the village. We have all day tomorrow to get ready. We will make a Christmas for the town. Everyone sit still now and let me think."

Early the next morning, Jingle went to the village square and put up a sign. The mayor came out of his house.

"Oh, *piccolo pagliaccio*"—little clown—the mayor said. "You are kind, but we can't have a circus this year. We are too poor."

"But Signor Mayor, it says it's free," Signora Lena said.

"But it also says it's in the town square, and it is starting to snow," Pietro pointed out. "You won't be able to perform here tonight."

"It will be all right. I know it will," Jingle said. "Please come."

IL
CIRCO PICCOLO
~ PRESENTS ~
·A·SPECIAL·
·CHRISTMAS· EVE·
·SHOW·

ADMISSION: FREE
TIME: TONIGHT
PLACE: TOWN SQUARE

"Ah, Jingle," Donna Chiara said when Jingle told her what he and the animals were going to do. "You have such a big heart, *caro mio*. I shall help too. I can sew your costumes!"

Donna Chiara sat and sewed while Jingle rehearsed with the baby animals. Outside, snow fell all day long.

"I know it will be all right," Jingle kept telling himself. "I know in my heart. We mustn't give up. Now once more. . . ."

"It's time, everyone!" Jingle stepped out of the tent. The night took his breath away. The snow had stopped and the stone streets sparkled with white. Stars, looking like diamonds flung up by a giant hand, twinkled in the deep-blue velvet sky.

Donna Chiara walked to the town square with Jingle and his troupe.
Lolly swept away the snow in a big circle. Sparkle and Pita packed
it down with their hooves. The monkeys climbed all over the place
putting up ropes.

"Time to put on our costumes," Jingle called.

Next he took the instruments out of the trunk and gave them to the monkeys. Then the little troupe marched around the square, banging the drums and tooting horns. Donna Chiara knocked on doors and shutters.

Slowly, one after another, shutters opened, and then doors. The villagers came out of their houses and Jingle's circus began.

Arfur and Bowsie jumped on and off Sparkle and Pita as they trotted around. Lolly danced. Simbo and Rana jumped through the hoops. The monkeys swung on ropes and trapezes. And Jingle tumbled better than he had ever tumbled before. The audience clapped and cheered.

"And now, friends, our finale," Jingle announced proudly.

The baby animals formed a pyramid. Jingle gave each of them a candle, and there in the middle of the square stood a living Christmas tree.

One by one the villagers went into their houses and put lighted candles in their windows.

"Look, look," the old people whispered, and pointed to the pyramid. The Christmas angel had appeared at the top of the living Christmas tree.

The angel opened its hands and golden stars fluttered down.

"*Buon Natale,*" the angel sang.

"*Buon Natale*"—Merry Christmas—the villagers sang back.

And when they looked at Jingle and the baby animals to thank them for their gift of Christmas, there, shining over Jingle's heart, was one of the golden stars.

Donna Chiara's Stelline d'Oro

created by Mary Ann Esposito, host of Ciao Italia,
the public television cooking program

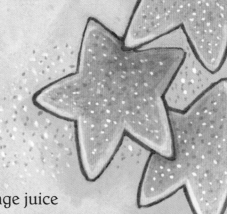

2 cups unbleached flour

½ tsp salt

½ tsp baking powder

½ cup butter or margarine

1 cup sugar

1 large egg

1 ½ tbsps orange flower water or 2 tbsps orange juice

◇ Sift the dry ingredients together and set aside.

◇ Cream the butter or margarine with the sugar. Add the egg, the orange flower water (or orange juice), and mix. Add to the dry ingredients and mix well.

◇ Wrap the dough in wax paper or plastic wrap and chill for at least 1 hour.

◇ Cut the dough into 4 pieces. Roll out each piece, one at a time, until ⅛" thick. Cut with small star cookie cutter. Place cookies evenly spaced on a large greased cookie sheet.

◇ Bake in a preheated 375°F oven for about 6–7 minutes. Watch carefully or cookies will begin to brown. They should be firm to the touch but still pale. Cookies will crisp as they cool.

◇ Carefully move cookies to a rack to cool. Continue with the dough until all is used. Makes 4–5 dozen.

◇ When cookies are cool, ice with the following frosting:

⅛ tsp saffron threads or powdered saffron

1 ½ tbsps warm water

1 ½ tbsps orange flower water or orange juice

1 cup confectioners' sugar, sifted

◇ Soak saffron threads for at least 10 minutes in the warm water; strain the liquid so it is clear and discard threads. (If using the powdered saffron, dissolve in warm water.) Add the saffron water and the orange flower water or orange juice to the confectioners' sugar. Mix well. Frost cookies and sprinkle with coarse raw sugar or Hundreds & Thousands.